The Little RED HEN

A FAVORITE FOLK-TALE

Pictures by J. P. Miller

🌷 A GOLDEN BOOK • NEW YORK

Copyright © 1954, renewed 1982 by Random House, Inc. All rights reserved. Published in the
United States by Golden Books, an imprint of Random House Children's Books, a division of
Random House, Inc., New York. Originally published in 1954 by Simon and Schuster, Inc.,
and Artists and Writers Guild, Inc. GOLDEN BOOKS, A GOLDEN BOOK, A LITTLE GOLDEN BOOK,
the G colophon, and the distinctive gold spine are registered trademarks of Random House, Inc.
A Little Golden Book Classic is a trademark of Random House, Inc.
www.goldenbooks.com
www.randomhouse.com/kids
Educators and librarians, for a variety of teaching tools, visit us at www.randomhouse.com/teachers
Library of Congress Control Number: 00-109697
ISBN: 978-0-307-96030-6
Printed in the United States of America
60 59 58 57 56 55

One summer day the Little Red Hen found a grain of wheat.

"A grain of wheat!" said the Little Red Hen to herself. "I will plant it."

She asked the duck:
"Will you help me plant this grain of wheat?"
"Not I!" said the duck.

She asked the goose:
"Will you help me plant this grain of wheat?"
"Not I!" said the goose.

She asked the cat:
"Will you help me plant this grain of wheat?"
"Not I!" said the cat.

She asked the pig:
"Will you help me plant this grain of wheat?"
"Not I!" said the pig.

"Then I will plant it myself," said the Little
Red Hen. And she did.

Soon the wheat grew tall, and the Little Red Hen
knew it was time to reap it.

"Who will help me reap the wheat?" she asked.

"Not I!" said the duck.

"Not I!" said the goose.

"Not I!" said the cat.

"Not I!" said the pig.

"Then I will reap it myself,"
said the Little Red Hen.
And she did.

She reaped the wheat, and it was ready to be taken to the mill and made into flour.

"Who will help me carry the wheat to the mill?" she asked.

"Not I!" said the duck.
"Not I!" said the goose.
"Not I!" said the cat.
"Not I!" said the pig.

"Then I will carry it myself," said the Little Red
Hen. And she did. She carried the wheat to the mill,
and the miller made it into flour.

When she got it home, she asked, "Who will help
me make the flour into dough?"

"Not I!" said the duck.

"Not I!" said the goose.

"Not I!" said the cat.

"Not I!" said the pig.

"Then I will make the dough myself," said the
Little Red Hen. And she did.

Soon the bread was ready to go into the oven.

"Who will help me bake the bread?" said the
Little Red Hen.

"Not I!" said the duck.

"Not I!" said the goose.

"Not I!" said the cat.

"Not I!" said the pig.

"Then I will bake it myself," said the Little
Red Hen. And she did.

After the loaf had been taken from the oven, it
was set on the windowsill to cool.

"And now," said the Little Red Hen, "who will help me eat the bread?"

"I will!" said the duck.

"I will!" said the goose.

"I will!" said the cat.

"I will!" said the pig.

"No, I will eat it myself!" said the Little Red
Hen. And she did.